Disney's THE HUNCHBACK OF NOTRE DAME

Adapted by Justine Korman

Illustrated by Don Williams

 A GOLDEN BOOK • NEW YORK

Western Publishing Company, Inc., Racine, Wisconsin 53404

Once upon a time, in the city of Paris, a young man lived in the bell tower of Notre Dame cathedral. He was strong enough to ring the giant church bells, but he was also so gentle he could hold a young bird in his hand.

His only friends were three gargoyles. They didn't mind his misshapen features that had led his cruel master to give him the name Quasimodo, meaning "half-formed."

Quasimodo knew nothing of the world below, except
what his master, Judge Frollo, told him. Frollo was a mean
man who hated everyone, especially the gypsies. He had
even taught Quasimodo to think of himself as a monster.

Quasimodo longed to see the world. But Frollo wouldn't let him leave the bell tower. "Out there people will hate you for being a monster," the cruel judge told him. This was Quasimodo's great sorrow, for he wanted so much to join the crowds in the streets of Paris.

Once a year everyone in Paris celebrated the Festival of Fools. On that topsy-turvy day, his gargoyle friends encouraged Quasimodo to climb down from the tower and join in the fun. During the Festival of Fools, many people wore masks, so no one paid any attention to Quasimodo's looks.

At the festival, Quasimodo saw a gypsy dancer named Esmeralda. He had never seen anyone so beautiful. Neither had Frollo's newest soldier, Captain Phoebus.

Then, before Quasimodo knew what was happening, he was pushed up on a stage where he was crowned the King of Fools. The crowd cheered and paraded him through the streets.

They brought Quasimodo to a platform in front of the
cathedral. Suddenly, some soldiers began to make fun of him.

"He's hideous! A monster!" they jeered, just as Frollo had
warned they would.

The crowd threw ropes over Quasimodo so he couldn't get
away.

Quasimodo saw Frollo in the crowd. "Master! Please help me," he begged.

But Frollo refused. He wanted to teach Quasimodo a lesson.

Gentle Esmeralda set Quasimodo free. "You mistreat this poor boy just as you mistreat my people," she said to Frollo. Then she tossed the King of Fools' crown at Frollo's feet.

"You will pay for this!" Frollo fumed. "Captain Phoebus, arrest her!"

But Esmeralda and her goat, Djali, sneaked into Notre Dame. Captain Phoebus followed them and advised Esmeralda to claim sanctuary. As long as she was inside a church, no one could arrest her.

"Set one foot outside these walls and you're my prisoner!" Frollo declared.

Quasimodo was confused. Frollo had told him all gypsies were evil. But Esmeralda was kind and good. She did not think Quasimodo was a monster. "Maybe Frollo is wrong about both of us," Esmeralda said.

Quasimodo decided to help her escape.

Very quietly Quasimodo carried Esmeralda and Djali down the cathedral walls.

Esmeralda pressed a special amulet into Quasimodo's hand. "Use this if you ever need help," she said. "It will help you find the gypsy hideout—the Court of Miracles." Then she kissed Quasimodo on the cheek and promised to visit him again.

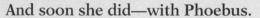

And soon she did—with Phoebus.

When Esmeralda had escaped, Frollo was furious. All the gypsies suffered as he tried to find her. Only Phoebus was brave enough to refuse to harm them—and he was badly wounded for defying Frollo.

"Please hide Phoebus here until he's strong again," Esmeralda pleaded.

Quasimodo could see that Esmeralda loved the handsome soldier. He wished she loved him instead, but he agreed to keep Phoebus safe in the bell tower.

Djali bleated a warning, and Quasimodo saw that Frollo was coming into the cathedral. "You must go!" he told Esmeralda.

"Please promise to keep Phoebus from harm," Esmeralda said before she hurried away.

"I promise," Quasimodo replied.

Frollo thought Quasimodo might know where to find
Esmeralda and the other gypsies. "I know where her hideout is,"
he told Quasimodo. "I attack at dawn with a thousand men."
But it was a trick!

Quasimodo and Phoebus rushed to warn the gypsies. Using Esmeralda's amulet, they found the Court of Miracles. But Frollo's men had been secretly following them! The hateful judge finally had caught up with all the gypsies.

"Take them away!" Frollo cried.
Quasimodo fell at his master's feet. "No, please!" he begged.
But Frollo's heart was as hard as the stones of Notre Dame.

The next day Quasimodo was chained high in the cathedral. In the square below, Frollo threatened to punish Esmeralda.

"Noooo!" Quasimodo cried. He strained at his chains until the tower shook, the bells rang, and the stones cracked. Then he scrambled down the walls to free Esmeralda. Quasimodo carried her back up to safety in the cathedral.

"Break down the door!" Frollo commanded. But Phoebus and the people of Paris would not let anyone hurt their beloved Notre Dame. The gargoyles also helped Quasimodo defend the church against Frollo and his men.

At long last Frollo's evil reign had ended. Quasimodo heard
the crowd cheer, "Hip, hip, hooray for Quasimodo!"

Finally he understood that he wasn't a monster at all. To the
people of Paris, Quasimodo was a great hero!